I0606994

Wilmot Proviso Brush

Brand Book

Wilmot Proviso Brush

Brand Book

ISBN/EAN: 9783337724719

Printed in Europe, USA, Canada, Australia, Japan

Cover: Foto ©Andreas Hilbeck / pixelio.de

More available books at **www.hansebooks.com**

1882.

ᒍRAND BOOK

Containing the Brands of the

CHEROKEE STRIP,

AUTHORIZED BY

STOCKMEN'S CONVENTION,

HELD AT

CALDWELL, KANS., MARCH 1 AND 2, 1882.

ALSO, THE BRANDS OF THE

Southwestern Cattle - Growers' Association,

ORGANIZED AT

MEDICINE LODGE, KAS., MARCH 17 & 18, 1882.

W. PROVISO BRUSH,
Compiler and Publisher

KANSAS CITY, MO.
ISAAC P. MOORE, PRINTER AND BINDER.
1882.

PREFACE.

It is perhaps due the Committee and patrons, that some statement be made by the publisher of this book. The unforseen delays in receiving copy, some of which had to be returned for correction, and the inexperience of workmen in this special kind of bookwork, may have occasioned and left some uncorrected errors, which were unavoidable. Hoping that the book as it is may give general satisfaction, and merit a continuance of your confidence and esteem, I am,

Your Obediant Servant,

W. P. Brush.

INDEX.

—TO—

BRANDS CHEROKEE STRIP.

M. H. BENNETT.

Post-office address, Caldwell, Kansas. Range, Saltfork, I. T. Cattle branded ⊞ or H on both sides; some branded ∽ on right side and ⊞ on left side.

Horse brand, same as this cut.

BENNETT & OVERALL.

Post-office address, Caldwell, Kansas. Range Pond Creek, I. T. Cattle brand same as cut and — on right hip; under half crop left ear.

Horse brand ✚ on right shoulder.

WM. C. QUINLAN.

Post-office address, Kansas City, Mo. Range, Cimarron River. Cattle brand same as cut.

Horse brand, same on left shoulder.

Other brands, on cattle, anywhere ⅂L on animal; also ⅂5 on both hips.

KANSAS CITY CATTLE COMPANY.

Post-office address, Kiowa, Kansas., and Kansas City, Mo.

Range, Eagle Chief Creek. All cattle branded same as cut, on both sides.

Horse brand, same as cattle, on left shoulder.

Other brands: I on both sides.

EEN. S. MILLER.

Post-office address, Caldwell, Kas.

Range, Big Sandy and Salt Fork.

Cattle brand, same as cut.

Horse brand, same as cut, on right hip.

Other brands, circle bar I, and YZ.

BLAIR, BATTIN & COOPER.

Post-office address, Caldwell, Kas.

Range, Salt Fork, I. T., seven miles west of Pond Creek Ranch. Cattle brand, same as cut. Horse brand, S on left hip. Other brands, Cattle are all branded on both sides with the S.

B. F. BUZARD.

Post-office address, St. Joseph, Mo.

Range, on East Sand Creek. Cattle brand same as cut.

Horse brand, same as on cattle.

E. M. HEWINS & CO.

Post-office address, Hunnewell, Kansas. Range, Pond Creek, I. T. Cattle brand, same as cuts. Horse brand, same as cattle brand, anywhere on the animal.

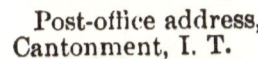

DICKEY BROS.

Post-office address, Cantonment, I. T.

Range, North Canadian River. Cattle brand, same as cut. Most all cattle branded on both sides.

Horse brand, same as cattle brand; some-

times on left hip, sometimes on left shoulder.

A. M. COLSEN.

Post-office address, Caldwell, Kas.

Range, Crooked Creek, I. T. Cattle brand, same as cut.

Horse brand, Ox Yoke on left shoulder. Other brands: All cattle branded on both sides or hips with Ox Yoke.

DRUMM & SNIDER.

Post-office address, Kiowa, Kas. Range, Mouth of Medicine River. Cattle brand, same brand as cut, some branded like cut, anywhere on animal.

Horse brand, same as cattle brand, on left shoulder.

CARNEGIE & FRAISER.

Post-office address, Pond Creek, I. T. Range, on Coldwater, I. T. Cattle brand, same as cut. Additional brands (principally on left side or hip): 55; Z; 7; H; J H; ⊢ and H ; ☓ and H ; ✝ ; OR.

Horse brand, same as cut without the T.

CEPHAS MILLER.

Post-office address, Caldwell, Kas. Range, Salt Fork. Cattle brand, same as cut. Horse brand, X on left shoulder, 11 on left side.

RICHARDS & SACRA.

Post-office address, Gainesville, Texas. Range, Turkey creek, I. T. Cattle brand, same as cut. Horse brand, same as cattle brand, on left hip.

Other brands \

—— on cattle.

STOLLER & REES.

Post-office address, Pond Creek, I. T.

Range, Salt Fork, I. T. Cattle brand, same as cut. Horse brand, XS on left shoulder.

Other brands, on cattle, —SX on left side; also, 4X4 on left side.

W. E. CAMPBELL.

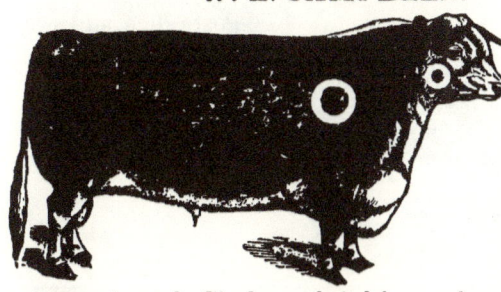

P. O. address, Caldwell, Kas.

Range, in Medicine River and Sand Creek Pool. Cattle brand, same as cut.

Horse brand, Circle on left hip or shoulder. Other brands, (on cattle), Perpendicular Bar on both cheeks and shoulders; also Circle road brand on one or both sides or back; also Circle on left jaw and shoulder.

W. E. Campbell, breeder of Thoroughbred and High Grade Hereford and Short Horn Cattle, Caldwell, Kas. Ranch, at the State Line, on Little Sandy. Cattle branded O on both cheeks and shoulders. O on left shoulder or I on both cheeks and shoulders. Marked underneath in each ear. Also, the road brand, O on one or both sides, or I on left cheek and shoulder. Horse brand, O on left hip or shoulder. Fine Bulls for sale.

PETER STEWART.

Post-office address, Wellington, Kas.

Range, Red Rock, I. T. Cattle brand, same as cut. Horse brand, same as cattle brand, on left shoulder. Other brands, same brand, on both sides; some same brand on left side or hip, and some branded with 1 on left hip; some, 111 on left hip or side.

C. M. McCLELLAN.

Post-office address Oto Agency, I. T. Range, Lower Black Bear. Cattle brand, same as cut. Different ear marks.

Horse brand, CM on left shoulder.

A. ADAMS.

Post-office address, Chetopa, Kas.
Range, Red Fork, I. T. Cattle brand, same as cut.

A. P. ATTERBERY.

Post-office address, Caldwell, Kansas. Range, Crooked Cr'k, I. T. Above brand on either side and bar on either hip.

F. & F. M. DAVIS.

Post-office address, Anthony, Kas.
Range, Big Sandy. Other brands, known as F. D. connected, anywhere on animal.

H. A. LATHAM,

Post-office address, Anthony, Kas.

Range, Big Sandy, I. T.

Above brand any where on left side or hip. Other brands, known as hat brand.

JOS. SLAUGHTER,

Post-office address, Chetopa, Kas.

Range, Red Fork, Ind. Ter.

J. C. BUTTS,

Post-office address, Bluff Creek, Harper Co., Kas.

Range. Crooked Creek. Horse brand, Cross on right shoulder. Other brands, Cross-B-cross on right side and some

on left side and some B on left.

GEORGE F. SMITH,

Post-office address, Keosaqua, Iowa.

Range, Pond Creek, Ind. Ter.

F. A. SANBORN,

Post-office address, Pawn Creek, I. T. Range, Wagon Creek.
Horse brand, Anchor on left shoulder. Other brands, Anchor reversed and Anchor on right side.

L. E. ROCK,

Post-office address, Pawn Creek, I. T. Range, Wagon Creek.
Horse brand, half diamond R on left hip.

H. DONOVAN,

Post-office address, Kiowa, Kas. Range, Barber County, Kas.
Horse brand, H D on right shoulder. Other brands, H D on both isdes of cattle.

CHAS. G. WALL,

Post-office address, Caldwell, Kas.
Range, with, B. F. Buzard.
Horse brand, as on cattle.

S. COOPER,

Post-office address,
Altamont, Ill.

Range, Dry Creek;
in charge of W. T.
Cooper, Hunnewell,
Kas.

WALTER E. TREADWELL,

Post-office address,
Anthony, Kas.

Range, Circle Bar.
Above brand on the
side or hip; ear mark,
under seven in left
ear. Other brands,
Thoroughbred and
High Grade Cows are
marked with metal
label or tab in left
ear, bearing number
of cow, name and
address. Walter E.
Treadwell, "Prospect
Park," Kas.

Some take Prospect
Park, and some An-
thony, Kas.

J. C. PRYOR & CO,

Post-office address,
Anthony Kas.

Ranch, on Sand
Creek, I. T. Cattle
brand, P diamond on
right hip of cattle,
except last spring's
calves, which are
branded P diamond
on right side and dia-
mond on left hip.
Ear mark, Crop off left ear and under-crop off right
ear. Horse brand, Diamond on left shoulder.

T. F. PRYOR & CO,

Post-office address, Anthony, Kas.

Ranch, on Sand Creek, I. T. Cattle brand, C on each shoulder and bar — on each side of neck, Ear mark, Under-hack in each ear. Horse brand, C on right shoulder.

D. T. BEALS,

Post-office, address, Caldwell, Kas. Range, in Pan Handle of Tex-as. Horse brand, same as cattle brand, on left shoulder.

Other brands on cat. tle, X on left hip or side ; also ∧ and V on left side or hip.

BEN GARLAND,

Post - office address, Caldwell, Kas. Range, Pond Creek, I. T.

Horse brand, same as cattle, on left hip. Other brands, on cat-tle, ∧ on either or both sides; also 7L on left hip.

L. BANKS WILSON,

Post-office address, Caldwell, Kas.

Range, Turkey Creek, I. T. Horse brand, same as cattle brand.

W. B. HELM,

Post-office address, Hunnewell, Kas.

Range, Thompson's Creek. Horse brand, II on right thigh; also, H on right hip. Other brands, of cattle, 10 on right side or hip; also O-▷ and ⊖ on left side; also H on left side, hip or loin.

THEO. HORSLEY

Post office address, Hunnewell, Kas.

Range, Chikaskia and Bitter Creek.

Horse brand, Cross on shoulder.

Other brands, T on hips; also, T on sides; also ⊏ and T on sides.

L. C. BIDWELL,

Post-Office address, Anthony, Kans.

Range, Big Sandy, I. T. Above brand anywhere on animal.

Horse brand, same as cattle, on left hip.

J. M. DAWSON,

Post-Office address, Fort Worth, Tex.

Range, Buffalo Creek. Horse brand, ┌ on left shoulder. Other brands on cattle, U on hip, J+ on side, ┐┐L on side, ♀ on hip, ♀ on side and shoulder, PEL on side.

J. P. JACKSON,

Post-office address, Pond Creek, I. T.

Range, south of Salt Fork.

Horse brand, JJ on left hip.

Other brands, snake without J.

TIMBERLAKE & HALL,

Post-office address, Kiowa, Barber Co. Kas. Range, 20 miles south of Drumms, I.T. With or without bar anywhere on animal.

Horse brand, without bar. Other brands, Ear mark, over bit and under hack each ear.

WINDSOR BROS.

Post-office address, Pond Creek, I.T. and Wichita, Kan.

Range, Salt Fork. Horse Brand, WIN on left hip. Other brands, V on left loin.

F. E. BATES & CO.

Post-office address, Caldwell, Kan.

Range, Sand Creek, I. T. Same as cut, on either or both sides of cattle.

Horse brand, same on left shoulder.

A. L. RAYMOND,

Post-office address, Caldwell, Kas. Range, Indian Creek, I. T.

Horse brand, same as cattle. Other brands M L ᴅ̄ on left side.

L. MUSGROVE,

Post-office address, South Haven, Kans. Range, Polecat creek, I. T. Horse brand, U on right shoulder. Other brands, also U on right side, and I on loin, also ⊃ on right side, also ⌐ on left side and ON on same side.

GEO. W. GORTON,

Post-office address, Harper Kans.

Horse brand, G on left shoulder. Other brands, on cattle G on right side; also G on right side,

BRIDGE & DRAPER,

Post-office address, Caldwell, Kas.

Range, Little Sand Creek, south of Salt Fork. Horse brand, △ on right shoulder. Other brands, △ on both sides; some D on both hips.

GREGORY, ELDRED & CO.,

Post-office address, Medicine Lodge, Ks. Range, Cimarron and Salt Fork.

Horse brand, Ɛ on hip or shoulder.

Other brands, Ŧ anywhere on animal.

Ear mark, crop off left, under-bit in right.

JOHN NICHOLSON,

Post-office address, Caldwell, Kas.
Range, with B. F. Buzard.
Horse brand, same as on cattle.

H. O'BRIAN,

Post-office address, Kiowa, Kas. Range, Driftwood, I. T.
Horse brand, ⌐ TI.
Other brands, on cattle, TI on either side.

WILSON & ZIMMERMAN.

Post-office address, Skeleton Ranch, I.T.
Range, Skeleton Creek, I. T.
Horse brand, ⚌ on left shoulder.
Other brands, ✚ ⚌, both brands on left side. ✚ D on left side, ⋀ on left side, U on both sides.

WILSON & ZIMMERMAN,

Post-office address, Skeleton Ranche, I. T. Range, Skeleton creek, I. T.

Horse brand, $=$ on left shoulder.

Other brands, on cattle, 8 on left side, 8 ∞ on right side and hip, $\bigcirc\!\!-$ on left side, $-\!\!- \; -\!\!-$ on ther side, jinglebob ear mark

E. M. FORD,

Post-office address, Hunnewell, Kas. Range, Red Rock creek, I. T.

Horse brand 4D on left shoulder, and $\heartsuit$ on left hip.

Other brands, $\frown$

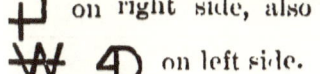

on right side, also P. C. $\bigcirc$. JY. ZN. $\heartsuit$

$\not\!\!\perp$ $\bigforall$ 4D on left side.

H. L. BICKFORD,

Post-office address, Cantonment, I. T.

Horse brand, same as cattle, on left shoulder.

Other brands, on cattle $+$ behind left shoulder.

CHAS. COLLINS,

Post-office address, Hutchinson, Kas. Range, Ash Grove, I. T. Brand on both sides. Horse brand, ᴝ on left hip.

J. C. HENDERSON & CO.,

Post-office address, Ponca Agency, I. T. Range, South of Bear Creek, I. T.

Horse Brand, [on left hip. Other brands, O U R on left side, and F S on left hip, and various other brands shown by bill of sale given at purchase of cattle.

BARNES & LEISS,

Post-office address, Caldwell, Kas. Range, Osage Cr'k, I. T. Cattle branded on both hips.

A. McLAIN, "Agent,"

Post-office address, Caldwell, Kas. Range, Red Rock, three miles east of Hunnewell trail. Horse brand, same as cattle. Other brands, on yearlings and calves, both ears split.

LIBBY & MOODY.

Post-office address, Maple City, Kas. Range, Red Rock. Horse brand, same as on cut, on left shoulder. Other brands, hat brand up side down, on right jaw: 7 on both hips and both jaws.

C. H. MANNING,

Post-office address, Caldwell, Kas.

Range Crooked Creek, I. T. Horse brand, same as on cut, on left shoulder. Other brands, 11, on left side ; 11 on right side ; 111 right hip ;

G 9 on right

de ; I V on left side ; V I on left side ; V

1 left side, some on right ; R S on right side.

ᎱARRETTSON & BERGIN,

Post-office Address, Kansas City, Mo.

Range, Sand Creek, twenty miles south Drumms. Brand on either side of animal. Horse brand, same, on left shoulder.

EWELL BROS.,

Post-office address, Kiowa, Kas. Range, Salt Fork and Eagle Chief Pool, I. T.

Horse brand, U on left shoulder.

Other brands, U

C ᐱ on cattle on both sides.

A. S. C. FORBES,

Post-office address, Caldwell, Kas.

Range, Turkey Creek.

Horse brand, inverted B on right shoulder. "ᗺ"

DENNIS DONVAN.

Post-office address, Kiowa, Barber Co., Kas.

Range, Driftwood. Horse brand, XT

Other brands, the old herd branded X T on right and left loin.

SMITH & LEE,

Post-office address, Caldwell, Kas.

Range, Indian Cr'k, I. T. Some cattle br'd'd K over bar on left side. Horse brand $\mathcal{N}$ on right shoulder. Other brands, on cattle 1S1, and Ω on left side.

ROB'T ETOCK,

Post-office address, Caldwell, Kas.

Range, Turkey Creek. Horse brand, same as cattle, on left hip.

W. S. MENDENHALL,

LEWIS CONRAD, Agent,

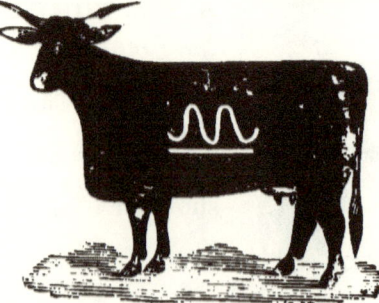

Post-office address, Winfield, Kas.

Brand, with bar under on either side or hip.

Horse brand, same on either shoulder or hip.

M. K. KRIDER,

Post-office address, Anthony, Kas.

Range, Medicine River and Salt Creek Pool. Cattle brand as above, on both hips and sides.

Road brand, ♡ on left side. Other

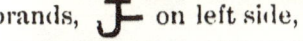

brands, ⅃ on left side, ⎩ on right side of same.

W. K. CLIFFORD,

Post-office address, Anthony, Kas.

Range, Medicine River and Salt Creek Pool. Road brand,

B̄ Q some animals T on both hips.

SHATTUCK BROS., PARKER & ROLANDS.

Post-office address, Pond Creek, I. T.

Range, Wild Horse.

Horse brand, same as cattle, on left thigh.

Other brands, this brand is on either side or hip.

SNOW & COOKSEY,

Post-office address, Caldwell, Kas.

Range, Red Rock. Horse brand, same as cattle, on left shoulder.

Other brands, on cattle branded ⋀K on both sides.

A. J. & C. P. DAY,

Post-office address, Cantonment, I. T.

Range, North Canadian River, I. T. Some cattle branded only on side. Horse brand, same as cattle, on left thigh.

CAMP LYNCH,

Post-office address, Pond Creek, I. T.

Range, Crooked Creek. Horse brand, same as cattle, on right hip.

Other brands, on cattle, C L on on left side and some branded ⊃ on left side.

Young cattle same as cut, both sides, and old cattle same on right side.

G. B. ROWDEN,

Post-office address, Cantonment, I. T.

Range, with A. J. & C. P. Day. Horse brand, same as cattle, on left thigh.

A. J. & C. P. DAY.

Post-office address, Cantonment, I. T.

Range, North Canadian River.

Horse brand, same on left thigh.

Other brands, **A** ⚓ on cattle.

A. T. & T. P. WILSON,

' Post-office, address, Kiowa, Kas.
ｉ Range, Drumm's Ranch, mouth of the Medicine River, I. T. Horse brand, same as cattle. Other brands, bar on left hip, thus, ＼ Ｑ anywhere on left side.

T. S. HUTTON,

Post-office address, Skeleton Ranch,I.T., via. Caldwall, Kas.
Range, Black Bear Creek, I. T. Horse brand, ♀ on left shoulder.
Other brands, cattle ♀ on left side,

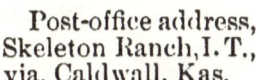 on left side, some L on the jaw and W on left side ⊖ on both sides.

L. B. HAVER,

Post-office address, Caldwell, Kas.
Range, Salt Fork, I. T.
Cattle branded on both sides as above.
Horse brand, ☐ on left shoulder.

M. J. LANE,

Post-office address, Kiowa, Barbour Co., Kas. Range, Salt Fork and Eagle Chief Pool. Horse brand, same, on left hip.
Other brands, cattle in various marks and other brands.

WM. FORBES,

Post-office address, Anthony, Kas.

Range, Crooked Creek, I. T. brand on both sides or hips.

Horse brand, JH .

Other brands, also F on both sides or hips, also some ⌐

⊤ on left side.

WILLIAM CORZINE,

Post-office address, Caldwell, Kas.

Range, on Osage Creek, I. T.

Horse brand, —— on left shoulder.

Other brands, same brand on right side of one lot; one lot branded IC on right side.

WILLIAMSON, BLAIR & CO.,

Post-office address, Pond Creek, I. T.

Range, Pond Creek and Salt Fork.

Horse brand, bar on each shoulder.

Other brands, same as above on both sides; some branded

℧

JAQUINS & BRADY,

Post-office address, Skeleton Ranch, I. T.

Range, Red Rock.

Cattle branded on shoulder or left side.

O. F. CASTEEN,

Post-office address, Anthony, Kas.

Range, Crooked Creek, I. T. Horse brand, OXO. Other brands, X—X on left side.

J. W. GLENN,

Post-office address, Hunnewell, Kas.

Cattle branded on both hips.

DEAN BROS.,

Post-office address, Arkansas City, Kas. Range, Otter Creek, I. T. Other brands, ㅍ on left side and D on left hip.

Horse, brand D on left shoulder.

Ear marks, under-half the left and crop in right.

JAMES A. HAMMERS & CO.

Post-office address, Anthony, Kas.

Range, Crooked Creek, I. T. Horse brand, ⨆ on right shoulder.

Other brands, ⋀⋀ T on left side and hip; L S on right side; ⨆ on right

de or hip, and on some ⨆∪ on right side or hip.

JOHN VOLZ,

Post-office address
Cantonment, I. T.
  Horse Brand, J V
on left shoulder.

A. R. YOUNG,

Post-office address
Caldwell, Kas.
  Range, with A. J
& C. P. Day, North
Canadian river, I. T

Horse brand,

O. H. P. McDOWELL.

Post-office address
Hunnewell, Kas.
  Range, on Polecat
I. T. Horse Brand
JF on right shoul·
der.   Other brands
McD on either side.
L.E on left side; also
P.H on left side ; H
on right side of same
cattle.

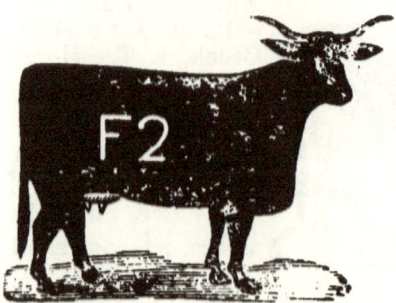

STROUT & FOSS

Post-offiice address
Hunnewell, Kas.
  Range, Bitter Cr
I. T.   Brand any·
where on right side,
Horse brand, same
on right hip or thigh

E. B. HARROLD & BROS.,

Post-office address, Archer City, Archer Co., Texas. Range, Three Forks Little Wichita River.

Horse Brand, same as this brand, on left shoulder.

Other brands, Cow brand, RO on left thigh and side; — F

— F on left side and hip, FAR F on left side and shoulder, ZZZ on left side and neck, TOX on left side and O on neck, half circle F on left side and shoulder, WIT on left side,

H on left side and thigh, X on

ioulder, and running M on left side and O on jaw, O on left shoulder and RO on left side. All these rands have various ear marks.

T. L. HILL,

Post-Office address, Morrilton, Arkansas. Range, with Houghton, R. II., Black Bear.

HARRIS & TOLLE.

Post-office address, Ponca Agency, I. T. Range, Black Bear, East Oklohoma road.

Horse brand 2 and

ℍℾ on left shoulder. Other brands, some of above brand 2 on right side.

A. HOBBS.

Post-office address,
Kinsley, Kas.
Horse Brand, same
as cattle on left hip.
Road Brand, △
anywhere on animal.

HENRY WISNER,

Post-office address,
Inyo, Kas. Range,
10 miles east of Medi-
cine Lodge, Kas.
Horse brand, W
on right hip, some
◊ on right shoul-
der.
Other brands H◊
on right side, and C on horns, C on neck and T on the
ft shoulder. Ranche Brand HW on right side.

L. P. ROBISON,

Post-office address,
Caldwell, Kas.
Range, Sand Creek,
I. T., Reno trail.
Ear mark, Crop
and split in right,
swallow fork in left
ear. Horse brand, if
any, ∧ Other
brands, same as above on either side; left horn sawed.

JOHNSONS & HOSMER,

Post-office address,
Arkansas City, Kas.
Range, Black Bear to
Cimarron, with R.
H. Houghton.
Other brands, Z on
right hip, F on left
hip. J X H brand is
5 inches.

HOUGTON & SPEERS,

Post-office address, Arkansas City, Kas. Range, Black Bear to Cimarron, East Oklohoma road.

Horse brand, on left shoulder.

Other brands, U or ∩ on left side or loin, △ on left hip,

⌐ just back left shoulder, — on left hip, L on t hip. The above are nearly all branded three es, about 5, 4½ and 3½ inches.

L. A. PICKERING.

Post-office address, South Haven, Kas. Range, Chikaskia. Other brand, some > on right side.

F. A. HUNT.

Post-office address, South Haven, Kas. Range, Chikaskia, Ear marks, crop off each and slit in left.

M. L. TROUT,

Post-office address, South Haven, Kas.

POWELL BROS. & ARNOLD.

Post-office address, Pond Creek, I. T.

Range, on Coldwater, Ind. Ter. Horse brand, 101 on left shoulder.

Other brands, 101 on right side and rail on left.

JOHN COOPER,

Post-office address, Pond Creek, I. T.

Range, on head of Wild Horse.

Cattle branded as above on either side hip or loin.

Horse brand same as cattle, on left shoulder.

J. H. GREENLEE.

Post-office address, Winfield, Kas.

Range, Red Rock, I. T. Other brands, —| O on left side.

WM. WYKES,

Post-office address, Caldwell, Kas.

Horse brand, same as cattle, on right or left shoulder.

A. HOPPESS,

Post-office address,
South Haven, Kas.

B. W. WARLOW & CO.,

Post-office address,
Caldwell, Kas.
Range, Pond Cr'k.
Same brand on
right side, laying
down.
Horse brand, $=$
on left side.

H. HODGSON,

Post-office address,
Pond Creek, I. T.
Range, Turkey
Creek, I. T.
Above brand on
either or both hips
or sides.
Other brands, ⌐
on right hip.

J. BOYD,

Post-office address,
Inyo post-office, Har-
per Co., Kas.
Range, on Little
Sandy, Barbour Co.
Horse brand, ℬ
on right shoulder.
Other brands, XN
on both sides; also,
road brands P R,
O C, B, ╫—, P J, J F, all on left side except the
J F, it on right side and hip.

J. L. KELLOGG.

Post-office address,
Wellington, Kas.
 Horse brand, same
cattle.

T. J. HOLCOMB,

Post-office address,
Anthony, Kas.
Range, Sand Creek,
I. T.
 The above brand
on both sides, some
laying, on either
side. Horse brand,
same, on right hip.

S. MANN,

Post-office address,
Wellington, Kas.

A. A. WILEY.

Post-office address,
Winfield, Kas.
Range, Red Rock,
I. T.
 Horse brand, S on
either shoulder.
 Other brands,

on left jaw,

on left side or hip.

H. M. SCOTT,

Post-office address, Chetopa, Kas.
Range, Red Fork, I. T.

W. W. WOODS,

Post-office address, Kiowa, Kas. Range, on Medicine, 10 miles south of Kiowa.

31 on left hip, both hips or both sides. Ear marks, crop off right, split in left.

Horse brand, the same. In addition to above, 16 head two-year-old bulls with bar under tail.

G. W. MILLER,

Post-office address, Hunnewell, Kans., Sylvester Flitch, in charge. Salt Fork Ranch. Brand, connected LK on left side.

N O on left side and 101 and brass knob on either of the horns. Also the following brands: JY on left side, T cross T on left side, IC on left loin, connected LK lying down on left loin, circle bar on both jaws, X on left side, LE on right side. Also **JW** on left hip, 11 on left side, X on left hip and dulaped. Horse brand, **K** on left shoulder.

A. H. JOHNSON,

Post-office address, Kansas City, Mo.

Range, Canadian River.

Other brands, ∧CE either side, ED on left side, with numerous other brands. For particulars, private brand book will be furnished free, by A. H. Johnson, No. 15 W. Missouri Avenue, Kansas City, Mo. Principal brand Adobe Wall Ranche HH either or both sides; owned by A. H. Johnson.

PRAIRIE CATTLE COMPANY.

Post-office address, 15 W. Missoure Ave., Kansas City, Mo.

Range, Cimarron, N. M. With or without tip on L. Horse brand, same as cattle. Other brands, L I T on right side, JJ on left hip, 7∧ on right side, L on right side and U on left shoulder, with other brands. Write to Prairie Cattle Co., 15 W. Missouri Ave., Kansas City, for private brand book.

MOORE & NYCE,

Post-office address, Caldwell, Kas. Range, Deer Creek, I. T.

Horse brand, same as cut, on left shoulder.

TERWILLIGER & DUTCHER,

Post-office address, Caldwell, Kas. Range, Deer Creek, I. T. Horse brand, T on left shoulder and D over bar on left hip.

QUINLAN & MONTGOMERY,

Post-office address,
Kansas City, Mo.
Range, Salt Fork,
Ind. Ter.

MONTGOMERY & OBERN,

Post-office address,
Kansas City, Mo.
Range, North Ca-
nadian, I. T.

SYNOPSIS OF PROCEEDINGS

OF THE

Stockmen of the Cherokee Strip,

HELD AT

CALDWELL, MARCH 1 & 2, 1882.

Meeting called to order by S. S. Birchfield, President.

Officers chosen for the ensuing year were, Ben. S. Miller, President, W. E. Campbell and H. C. Manning, Vice-Presidents, and M. H. Bennett, Treasurer.

On motion of W. E. Campbell, John A. Blair was elected Secretary, and W. P. Brush, of the Kansas City *Commercial Indicator*, Tell Walton, Caldwell *Post*, W. B. Hutchinson, Caldwell *Commercial*, T. A. McNeal, Medicine Lodge *Cresent*, Will Eaton, Cheyenne *Transporter*, and Joe Carter, Hunnewell *Independent*, Assistant Secretaries and honorary members of the Association.

The Treasurer, Mr. Bennett, was instructed to provide a register for the names and post-office address of each member, with instructions that such book be used as a reference book by the Association; and, on motion, the membership fee was increased to $1.00.

The Treasurer, Mr. Bennett, made his annual report for last year as follows:

Receipts from membership fees and advertising for brand book, $287. On expenditures for brand book of last year, $181, leaving a balance on hand in the treasury of $106.

Hon. E. M. Hewins moved that a committee of three take charge of publishing a brand book containing the brands of the Association. Motion adopted and chair appointed M. H. Bennett, Asa Overall and P. Carnegie as such committee.

Mr. Hewins moved that a committee of five be appointed on stock inspection, to appoint and employ an inspector for Kansas City, St. Louis and Chicago, and to report to the convention on Thursday.

E. M. Hewins, A. H. Johnson, W. Timberlake, Ben Garland and J. C. Pryor were appointed.

The following resolution was read by Secretary Blair and unanimously adopted:

Resolved, That the respective pool captains, and executive committees, notify the surrounding pools of any and all persons who have knowingly and willfully turned loose without their consent, or pay, or remuneration therefor, and that if said persons fail to pay, not only their assessments and proportion of the expenses, the established price for wintering cattle to the pool they turn loose with, on or before the 10th of April, 1882, they shall be denied the privilege of gathering cattle with any pool or members of this Association. And that the names of all persons, so refusing to pay, as aforesaid, be published in a dead-beat list in the Caldwell, Anthony and Medicine Lodge papers.

On motion, adjourned to meet at 10 o'clock A. M. Thursday.

THURSDAY—MORNING SESSION.

The meeting was called to order by President Miller, at 10 A. M.

The following communication was received and read by the President:

MEDICINE LODGE, KAS., February 27, 1882.

To our Friends and Co-workers, the Cattlemen, in Convention, at Caldwell, Greeting:

It is our sincere desire that you favor us with your presence at the meeting of the cattle men, to be held at Medicine Lodge on the 17th and 18th of March, 1882, and participate in the business proceedings, ball and banquet, on that occasion.

This done by order of committee.

W. F HOUGHTON,   E. W. PAYNE,
    Secretary.   Chairman.

Mr. Hewins moved that a vote of thanks be tendered the citizens of Medicine Lodge for the invitation. Carried.

Mr. T. F. Pryor then offered a resolution to the effect that a committee of three be appointed by the chair, to draft an address to the cattle drovers, embodying in it the resolution adopted by this Association, at its meeting in this city, March 17, 1881. The resolution was adopted, and the following named gentlemen appointed as such committee: W. E. Campbell, T. F. Pryor and W. S. Snow. The address is as follows:

TO TEXAS CATTLE DROVERS.

An Address to the Texas Cattle Drovers from the Southwestern Kansas and Indian Territory Stock Association.

At a meeting of the above named Association, held in the City of Caldwell, on the 1st and 2nd days of March, 1882, the following resolution, adopted at its meeting in March, 1881, was re-affirmed, and the undersigned appointed a committee to publish a suitable address in accordance therewith:

Resolved, That in order to prevent the spread of disease among the wintered cattle held on the Cherokee Strip, there ought to be established, and rigidly maintained, a proper line of separation and quarantine between through cattle and said wintered cattle; and that this convention recommend the establishment and maintenance of the following quarantine line, and request the active co-operation of the Cherokee Council and all stockmen driving through cattle into the Cherokee Strip, in maintaining said line. Osage Creek shall be the western boundary for through cattle; a line running east from Osage Creek, parallel with the northern boundary of the Nez Perces reservation, shall be the southern boundary for through cattle; the Arkansas River will be the eastern boundary for through cattle, and the State of Kansas shall be the northern boundary.

The undersigned, after careful consideration of the subject, do not deem any formal address necessary at this time, believing that every cattleman who will drive from Texas this year fully understands the situation of the cattle interests in the Territory and on the boundaries of Kansas, and will, so far as he can, use all due care to comply with the request of this Association, and respect the rights of those holding wintered and domestic cattle in the Territory.

The Association feel satisfied that the country selected as a holding ground for through cattle is of sufficient scope to furnish ample grazing for all cattle that may be driven to the Caldwell and Hunnewell markets. We would also state that the grounds selected are well adapted for grazing purposes, having a reasonable amount of timber, abundance of water, and are within easy reach of the stock yards at both Caldwell and Hunnewell.

Further than stating the above facts, we do not believe it necessary to dwell at length on this subject, feeling assured that our through cattle friends will fully appreciate the spirit in which the above resolution was adopted and this address put forth.

In conclusion, we assure all driving to the above named markets that the members of our Association will do all in their power to make their sojourn among us both pleasant and profitable.   Respectfully,
                              W. E. CAMPBELL,⎫
                              T. F. PRYOR,   ⎬ Committee.
                              W. S. SNOW,   ⎭

AFTERNOON SESSION.

Convention called to order at 2 P. M. by the Chairman.

The Committee on Inspection, by its Chairman, Mr. Johnson, offered the following report, and asked that the committee be discharged. Report read and approved, and committee discharged:

We, the undersigned committee, appointed at the convention of the stockmen of the Cherokee Strip, held March 1st, 1882, for the purpose of drawing up resolutions regarding inspection and assignments, recommend—

That this convention appoint Maj. A. Drumm, Jesse Evans and A. M. Colson, as a Standing Committee on Inspection, and give them full power to assess and collect in their divisions such amounts as in their judgment they may deem necessary to defray the expenses of inspection, not exceeding the sum of $5 per 1,000 head, and turn over all amounts of collection to the Treasurer of the Association; the committee to select one from their number, whose duty it shall be to draw amounts on the Treasurer for all expenses appertaining to inspection.

That they shall have the power to employ one inspector for Kansas City, one for St. Louis, and one for the Cheyenne and other Indian Agencies.

That they shall confer with the Committee of the Medicine Lodge Convention and be empowered to make such arrangements and take such action as they deem necessary to the interests of this convention.   A. H. JOHNSON,
                              E. M. HEWINS,
                              BEN GARLAND,
                              J. C. PRYOR.
                              W. H. TIMBERLAKE.

The Committee on Round-ups, by its Chairman, Mr. A. H. Johnson, asked leave to submit its report and be discharged from further consideration of the subject. Report received, read and approved, and the committee discharged.

We, the undersigned committee, appointed at the convention of the stockmen of the Cherokee Strip, held March 1, 1882, on round-ups, herewith submit the following report:

We recommend that the Territory known as the Cherokee Strip be divided into three divisions, to-wit:

Division No. 1 to be composed of what is known as the Red Fork and Salt Fork country, including the territory north of

there to the south line of the State of Kansas, and thence west,
including the Crooked creek and Sand creek country, on the
State line, to the east line of Comanche County Pool, said division to begin round-up at the crossing of Redrock creek on the
Arkansas City wagon road, and Abner Wilson to be appointed as
captain of said division; the day of the meeting of this division
to be decided upon by the committee appointed for that purpose.

Division No. 2 to be composed of the country lying south of
Division No. 1, as far south as the Cimmarron and west to the
line of the Barbour County Pool; this division to meet to begin
round-up where the Arkansas City wagon road crosses the Skele-
toncreek, and John Miller to be appointed captain of said division;
the day of meeting to be decided upon the same as in Division
No. 1.,

Division No. 3 to be composed of the country lying south of
Division No. 2 to the North Canadian river, thence west to the
western line of A. J. Day's ranch; said division to meet at
Caldwell or the Chisholm trail crossing of the North Canadian
river, and H. W. Timberlake to be appointed captain of said division; the day of meeting to be decided upon in the same man-
ner as the other divisions.

And we recommend that the captains of above divisions be
authorized to subdivide their respective divisions in such man-
ner as they deem advisable, and appoint captains for such sub-
divisions, but to retain absolute control of the same.

We recommend that the following named gentlemen, viz:
Maj. A. Drumm, M. K Krider, Oliver Ewell, H. W. Timberlake,
C. H. Manning and John A. Blair be appointed as the committee to set the time for each division to commence work, and
such time shall be set on or before the 18th day of March, and
shall be published in the Barbour. Harper and Sumner county
and Darlington papers, and that said committee confer with the
Barbour County Stock Association at their meeting on the 17th
day of March, and solicit their co operation in the coming
round-up.

A. H. JOHNSON,	J. A. BLAIR,
A. DRUMM,	JOHN REES,
W. E. CAMPBELL,	OLIVER EWELL,
MARION BLAIR,	J. MILLER,
H. W. TIMBERLAKE,	C. NELSON,
J. K. ZIMMERMAN,	J. NICHOLSON,
M. K KRIDER,	PAT. CARNEGIE,
C. F. PLOWMAN,	A. J. DAY,
JESSE EVANS,	W. E. QUINLAN.
SYLVESTER FLITCH,	J. W. CARTER,

JAS. MURRAY.

The following resolution was adopted:

Resolved, That the respective captains be empowered to dis-
charge all parties not doing satisfactory work, or refusing to
obey orders, and that the said captains be authorized to employ
other men to fill such vacancies, at the expense of the parties
who were represented by the parties so discharged.

Mr. E. M. Hewins offered the following resolution,
which was read and adopted without a dissenting
voice :

Resolved, That it is the sense of the stockmen and ranchmen
of this Association, that the six-shooter is not an absolute necessity and necessary adjunct to the outfits of cowboys working
on the ranges of the Cherokee Strip, and that we deprecate its
use, except in extreme cases of necessity while on duty in protecting the rights of property against Indians and outlaws; but
we deprecate the carrying of six-shooters in all cases while visiting the towns along the border.

On motion adjourned, subject to the call of the

OF THE

Southwestern Cattle Growers'

ASSOCIATION,

AS ORGANIZED AT

MEDICINE LODGE, KANSAS,

March 17 & 18, 1882.

This Division of the Book contains Brands belong-
ing to the Comanche County Pool, Barbour
County Stock Growers' Association,
and others, West and South.

INDEX.

SOUTHWESTERN ASSOCIATION

EVANS, HUNTER & EVANS,

Post-office address, Lake City, Kas.

Range, Comanche Co. Pool, Comanche Co. Kas.

Cattle branded on left hip or side. Ear mark, smooth crop off left ear and swallow fork in right. Old brand, rail brand and jingle-bob ear mark. Horse branded on left hip with heart brand. Other brands, cross and oblique bar on left side, jingle-bob in both ears. Also TF connected and rocking-chair, with various marks.

WM. BLAIR,

Post-office address, Lake City, Kas.

Range, Comanche Pool. Horse brand, Cross on left hip.

THOS. DORAN,

Post-office, address, Lake City, Kas.

Range, Comanche County Pool.

Ear mark, crop off the right and overbit in left. Horse brand, J on left hip.

C. D. NELSON,

Post-office address, Lake City, Kas.

Range, Comanche Pool. Brand on both hips. Ear marks, crop off each ear and under hack in both. Horse brand, same as cattle. Owned now by Hunter, Evans & Hunter.

R. W. PHILLIPS,

Post-office address, Sun City Kas.

Brand, same as cut on each side or left hip.

Additional brands, seventy - four connected on left hip. some stock. H H H on left neck, side and hip of some cattle.

Horse brand, seventy-four connected on left hip.

E. W. PAYNE,

Post-office address, Medicine Lodge, Ks.

Range, Comanche Pool. P on each hip or left loin. Ear mark, crop off each ear and underbit in left. Horse brand, P on left shoulder.

Other brands, HP connected, on each side.

R. KIRK, in Charge,

Post-office address, Larned, Kas.

Range, Comanche Co. Pool. Same as cut on both sides. Horse brand, same, on left hip.

JOHN WILSON,

Post-office address, Lake City, Kas.

Range, Comanche Co. Pool.

Horse brand, J on left shoulder.

Other brands. W on left hip.

J. B. DOYLE,

Post-office address, Evansville.

Range, Comanche Pool. Horse brand, JB connected on left hip.

Other brands, seven-six connected, on right side or neck. Ear marks, under bit right and under slope left.

J. M. RAWLINS,

Post-office address, Lake City, Kas.

Range, in Comanche Pool. Old stock, no ear marks.

Branded triangle R on left hip and I bar on right hip.

Horse brand, triangle R on left hip. Ear marks on young cattle, crop and under bit on left and split in right, same as cut.

C. W. JAMES, in Charge,

Post-office address, Lake City.

Same as cut, and half circle cross J on right hip.

Horse brand, half circle cross J on left hip. Other brands, 500 cross half and circle cross J, anywhere on animal.

J. A. McCARTY,

Post-office address, Lake City, Kas.

Range, Comanche Pool. Same as cut, on left hip and side. Horse brand, same as cattle, on left shoulder.

Ear marks, crop off right and over and under bit left.

W. R. COLCORD,

Post-office address, Lake City Kas.

Range, Comanche County Pool.

Horse brand, jug brand and XL connected, anywhere on animal.

Other brands, cross XL connected on left hip and COL on right side.

W. T. DAVIS,

Post-office address, Lake City, Kas.

On either side.

Additional brand, circle 5 on left hip.

Ear mark, under slope and upper bit.

Horse brand, same as cattle, on the left shoulder.

R. STEWART,

Post-office address, Kansas City, Mo.,

Range, Eagle Chief and Salt Fork Pool, I. T, Brand same as cut and S on left hip.

WEEKS BROS.,

Post-office address, Kinsley, Edwards Co., Kas. Range, Lone Tree, Clark Co., Kas.

Brand same as cut, on each hip.

Ear marks, sloping under bit in left, swallow fork and under bit in the right.

BRISBIN BROS.,

Post-office address, Medicine Lodge.

Range, Medicine River. Horse brand same as cattle.

Others brands, same as above and AK connected over bar and AK connected and cross.

TATUM BROS.,

Post-office address, Soldier Creek, Comache Co., Kas.

Range, head of Thompson Creek.

Horse brand, TH over bar on left thigh. Ranch brand, TH over bar, any-where on animal, ears split. Other brands, flying W, UO, AK, ON, all on left side, and TH, the flying W and UO are to be branded with TH over bar. The AK brand to be branded with TH.

EWING & POTTER,

Post-office address, Medicine Lodge.

Range, on Drift-wood, I. T.

Horse brand, same as cattle, on left shoul-der. Other brands, HK connected on left loin or left hip. The UI cattle branded on either or both sides.

W. P. Ewing, in charge.

FARRAR & BRO.

Post-office address, Soldier Creek, Co-manche C., Kas.

Range Thompson Creek. Horse brand 18 on left shoulder. Other brands, some cattle 18 on left jaw, 81 on left shoulder.

FRANK TOMLINSON,

Post-office address, Lake City, Barbour Co., Kas. Range, West Log Creek, 10 miles south of Lake City. Horse brand, same as cattle.

Other brands, D A connected, anywhere on animal and DAL on right side.   Ear mark, under bit in right and split in left.

C. BLACKSTONE,

Post-office address, Kiowa, Kas.

Range, I. T.

Cattle branded on both hips or sides known as reversed L and B connected.

Ear mark, crop off left and slit, and slit in right. Horse brand same as cattle.

CONNOR & TUCKER,

Post-office address, Kiowa, Kas. Range, Salty.

Horse brand, 5 on left shoulder.

Other brands, D bar, D5, 5.   Ear marks, crop and slit each ear.

GEORGE, KING & GEORGE,

Post-office address, Elm Mills, Barbour Co., Kas., or Wellington, Sumner, Co., Kas. Range on Upper Elm.   I or cross on left jaw.   Additional brands, V on left shoulder.   Cross 7 on right side.   Half circle I on left shoulder.   JAL on left side.

F. B. HUNT,

Post-office address, Medicine Lodge, Ks. Range, 5 miles n. w. on Medicine River.

Horse brand, same as cattle, on the left shoulder. Additional brand, HK disconnected over bar, anywhere on animal.

HALL BROS. & LOCKARD,

Post-office address, Medicine Lodge.

Range, Sand Creek and Hackberry Pool. Horse brand, O75.

Other brands, O75 on left side, HLO on side, connected, on right hip.

McKINNEY BROS.,

Post-office address, Lodi, Kas. Range, Sand Creek and Hackberry Pool.

Brand anywhere on animal. Additional brands, OX on left side, O on left side of neck, box and circle on left side ; crop and under bit in each ear.

Horse brand, WM on left hip.

S. W. STRONG,

Post-office address, Medicine Lodge, Barbour Co., Kas.

Ranch, on Upper Elm. Brand known as I bar anywhere on animal.

Horse brand, same, on either shoulder.

M. STRONG,

Post-office address, Medicine Lodge, Ks. Ranch, on W. Sand Creek. Known as the half circle bar brand, any place on animal. Also inverted half circle bar.

Horse brand, same, on either shoulder.

R. L. CARTER & CO.,

Post-office address, Elm Mills, Kas.

Known as the 6 H 9 brand, on both hips. In future will use this brand on the horn also.

THOMASON, CHRISMAN & PAYNE,

Post-office address, Medicine Lodge, Ks. Range, Cimarron River, I. T. Principal brand, seven-six connected ; part of stock branded on both sides, and some WF connected, on right side or hip.

Horse brand, seven-six connected, on left shoulder. Other brands, on young stock, O.T. Ear marks, crop off right and overbit in left. Crop off each ear on WF connected, calves.

H. H. WHITNEY & SON,

Post-office address, Medicine Lodge, Kas. Range, Salt Fork Pool. Other brands, — O —, 57, I K, bar each side and under O.

A. WATSON,

Post-office address, Soldier Creek, Kas. Brand on left side or hip. Ranche, at the mouth of Thompson Creek, on the Medicine, Comanche county. Additional brands, WK on left side, AK connected, over bar on left side. Horse brand, running W on left shoulder and hip.

W. H. HARRELSON,

Post-office address, Medicine Lodge, Ks., and Belton, Mo.

Range, Salt Fork and Eagle Chief pool

Above brand anywhere on animal, but principally on left side. Horse brand, reversed half circle bar on left shoulder.

Other brands, two half circles over bar anywhere on animal, but principally on left side.

IRA BOON,

Post-office address, Kiowa, Kas. Range, Driftwood.

Horse brand same as cattle, on left hip. Other brands, open A on left hip. Crop and two splits in left ear.

M. W. BRAND,

Post-office address, Kiowa, Kas. Range on Cimarron, with F. L. Mayhew & Son. Horse brand same, on left shoulder.

JOHN CURRY,

Post-office address, Inyo, Kas. Range, 10 miles east of Medicine Lodge. Horse brand, half circle C on right shoulder. Other brands, circle bar disconnected on right side and J on right hip. Some half circle U on right side and J on right hip. Some circle bar disconnected on right side and half circle U on left side. Ear mark, half of half under crop off right ear. New brand will be half circle C on right side and J on left hip.

J. P. ELSEA,

Post-office address, Lake City, Kas. Range, Bear Creek, twelve miles west of Medicine Lodge.

Horse brand, same as cattle on left shoulder.

Other brands, G — S and I N K on left side; J G on left side and hip.

J. P. ELSEA,

Some cattle branded same as cut on both sides.

W. J. ESTELL,

Post-office address, Lake City, Kas. Range, Big Mule, Comanche County.

Horse brand, same as on cattle, without bar. Other brands, on young stock, same brand on both sides and crop off right ear.

FINIS Y. EWING,

Post-office address, Kiowa, Kas. Range, Driftwood and Salt Fork. Horse brand, running N on left shoulder, on some U and running N on left shoulder. Other brands, Texas steers branded U and running N on both sides.

Cattle raised on Ranch are marked with dewlap crop in right and underbit in left ear.

J. A. LANE,

Post-office address, Sun City, Kas.

Range, Big Mule Creek, Comanche County Pool, Kas.

Horse brand, same as first cut, on left shoulder.

HOPPER BROS.

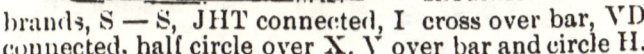

Post-office address, Sun City, Kas.

Range, Big Mule, mouth of Spring Creek. OC brand any part of animal. On both sides of all stock cattle. Horse brand, same, on left shoulder. Other brands, S — S, JHT connected, I cross over bar, VD connected, half circle over X, V over bar and circle H.

EDWARDS BROS. & BENEDICT.

Post-office address, Kinsley, Kas.

Range, head of the Medicine River, Comanche Co. Kas.

Horse brand, same, on left shoulder.

Other brands, A over bar on left hip, OL over bar on left hip or thigh, half circle over 7II on left side on hip, FS over bar on left side, HS on left side, JN on left side or hip, OL on left side with —— on shoulder, _Ω on both sides or hips. Ear marks, under and upperbit with crop on left.

C. H. DOUGLASS

Post-office address, Sun City, Kas.

Other brands, ⌐ on face on one or both hips or left side. Some of old brands are half circle L, and B C. Ear mark, jingle-bob in left ear.

A. W. INDERLAID.

Post-office address, Kinsley, Edwards Co., Kas.

Horse brand, ponies branded IS on left thigh and I on left side. Cattle in charge of Weeks Brothers until after round-up of 1882.

J. V. ANDREWS,

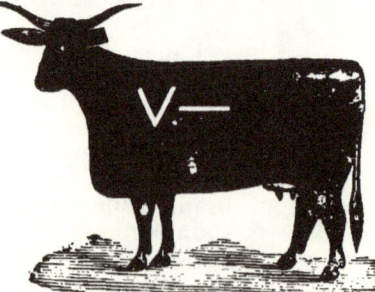

Post-office address, Camp Supply, I. T.

Range, Indian Territory. Horse brand, V bar and reel on left hip.

Other brands, reel ; also on some cattle, not yet in, V bar brand.

BALLENGER, SCHLUPP & WYETH,

Post-office address, Kiowa, Kas. Range, Salt Fork and Eagle Chief Pool. Other brands, 7 on left jaw; same as cut on any part of animal.

BALLENGER & SCHLUPP,

Post-office address, Kiowa, Kas.

Range, Salt Fork and Eagle Chief Pool.

Horse brand, S on left shoulder or hip. Other brands, S on left jaw. Brand on any part of ahimal.

C. C. MILLS, in Charge,

Post-office address, Red Creek, Kas.

Range, Salt Fork and Eagle Chief Pool. Horse brand, W cross on right shoulder. Other brands, running W 5 on left side.

GREEVER, HOUGHTON & CO.,

Post-office address, Medicine Lodge, Ks. Range Cimarron.

Same as cut on both sides.

Horse brand, 21 on left shoulder and left hip. Other brands, double circle on hip or side and long E on left side.

MILLS, SHERLOCK & CO.,

Post-office address, Lake City, Kas.

Range, Salt Fork and Eagle Chief Pool. Horse brand, 5L on right shoulder.

Other brands, 3L, MLS, HA connected over bar, 4L, circle on left hip and 2 on right hip.

STANDIFORD, YOUMANS & CO.,

Post-office address, Medicine Lodge, Ks. Range 6 miles south of Medicine Lodge.

Additional brands, half circle S, anywhere on animal; UT, anywhere on animal.

Arthur Gorham,

Post-office address, Kinsley, Kas. Range Cimarron river, west of the mouth of Buffalo. Brand on both sides and known as half circle box.

Horse brand, box.

Additional brand, box half circle.

N. G. ROWLEY,

Post-office address, Sun City, Kas. Range Sun City and Bear Creek Pool, Kas. 7Y on left shoulder; 7Y bar shot, both sides; both ears smooth crop. Horse brand, 7Y on left shoulder.

Other brands: old brands, open cross, inverted C and hat, 66, 6, VH connected, half circle Y and various other brands. All young cattle, like cut.

CONDENSED PROCEEDINGS

OF THE

Southwestern Cattle-Growers' Association,

HELD AT

MEDICINE LODGE, KAS., March 17 & 18, '82.

The stockmen organized as the SOUTHWESTERN CAT-
TLE GROWERS' ASSOCIATION, and elected officers for the
ensuing year, as follows:

E. W. PAYNE, President.

D. A. GREEVER, DAVID STITH and F. B. HUNT, Vice
Presidents.

W. F. HOUGHTON, Secretary.

W. W. COOK, Treasurer.

The Committee on Credentials were: Messrs. R. W.
Phillip, Comanche county; D. A. Greever, Cherokee
Strip; F. B. Hunt, Barbour county; Wash Mussett,
Indian Territory; A. Watson, Medicine Lodge; D.
Stith, Indian Territory, and Werk Randolf, Camp
Supply, who reported seventy-two persons for mem-
bership, and fixed the membership at $1.00.

The following resolution was adopted by the Association:

Resolved, That it is the sense of the stockmen and ranchmen of
the Cattle Growers' Association of the Southwest, that the six-
shooter is not an absolute necessity and necessary adjunct to the
outfit of cowboys working on the ranges of this Association, and
we deprecate its use except in extreme cases of necessity while
on duty, in protecting the rights and property against Indians
nd outlaws. And further, we condemn the habit of carrying
six-shooters by cowbows or others, especially while visiting any
of the towns along the border.

The Committee on Round-ups reported as follows.

That the general round-up parties shall meet at the several
respective places named below on the 7th of May, so as to pre-
pare to commence work on the following day under the manage-
ment of the captains appointed to take charge of these outfits.
The ranges to be worked by these outfits take in the stretch of
country lying between the North Canadian and the head of the
Medicine Rivers, which is to be worked from the East to the
West. This round-up party is to be divided into six separate
divisions.

The first division on the south is to meet and start from
Dickey's headquarters camp, seven miles west of Fort Cantonment, under the charge of C. F. Ploughman.

The second division to start from Ewell's headquarters camp,
on Eagle Chief, under the charge of Nick Sherlock.

The third division to start from W. E. Campbell's camp on
Sand Creek, under the charge of James Wilson.

The fourth division to start from Whitney's camp on Antelope
Flat, under the charge of John Mosley.

The fifth division to start from Bratton's ranch, on Elm Creek,
under the charge of Street Jones.

The sixth division to start from the mouth of Thompson's Creek, under the charge of S. H. Farrar.

[Signed by]

JESSE EVANS,   WM. LINDSEY.
DAVID STITH.   TONY DAY.
F. B. HUNT.   C. D. NELSON.
D. GREEVER.   CHAS. DOUGLASS.
L. WILSON.   NICK SHERLOCK.

Adopted.

The Committee on Brand Book recommended that the members of the Southwestern insert their brands in the Cherokee Strip Brand Book.   Adopted.

R. W. Phillips, ⎫
S. K. W. Field, ⎬ Committee.
R. T. Greer,   ⎭

The Committe on Inspection recommended, and was adopted, that Jesse Evans, S. K. W. Field and R. T. Greer, serve as a Standing Committee on Inspection, and that the Association give them full power to assess and collect such amount as in their judgment they may deem necessary to defray expenses of such inspection; provided, that such sum shall not exceed five dollars per thousand head.   The Committee to turn all moneys so collected over to the Treasurer of the Association.   The committee to select one of their number, whose duty it shall be to draw on the Treasurer for all amounts necessary to defray the expenses of inspection.   The Committee to have power to employ one inspector for Kansas City and one for the Indian Territory.   The inspector for Kansas City to be employed from the 1st of June to the 15th of November, and the one for the Indian Territory from November 1st to May 1st.

F. B. Hunt, ⎫
R. Kirk,   ⎬ Committee.
W. P. Ewing, ⎭

The following resolutions were passed:

Resolved, That all cows and calves be removed from the herd before cutting out the steers.

Resolved, That no herds be cut out and driven off the ranges without first having been inspected for strays.

Resolved, That we, members of the Cattle Growers' Association of the Southwest, do not think it just or our duty to go to the expense of gathering up all cattle held by parties within the jurisdiction of this Association other than those who have permanent ranches and co-operate with us.

Resolved, That we, the Cattle Growers of the Southwest, in convention assembled, do condemn the practice of turning cattle loose on the range without any effort to herd or take care of the same, and the practice of taking cattle on hire, where such increase of stock would infringe on the rights of adjoining cattlemen, as conduct unworthy any honorable cattleman.

Resolved, That all calves shall be branded in the marks of their dams when found on ranges not their own, and the same reported and published in the county papers.

Mr. Kirk moved that the present officers of the Association be made the Finance Committee on Brand Book.   Motion prevailed.

Adjourned, to meet at Medicine Lodge, November 15th, 1882.

John G. Woods, President.
F. A. Parsons, Cashier.

C. C. Curtis.
C. G. Larned.

BANKING HOUSE
—of—
WOODS, PARSONS & CO.
HARPER, KANSAS.

Do a General Banking Business. Give Special Attention to Stockmen and Collections. Fire-Proof Vaults, Burglar-Proof Safe and Time Lock.

W. W. COOK, LIVE STOCK BROKER,
Medicine Lodge, Kas.

Cattle Bought and Sold. | Correspondence Solicited.

LELAND HOTEL, CALDWELL, KAS.

Medicine Lodge House, MEDICINE LODGE, KAS.

WELLINGTON, KAS. — PHILLIPS HOUSE,

HUNNEWELL, KAS. — HUNNEWELL HOTEL,

1882	Sund.	Mond.	Tuesd.	Wedn.	Thurs.	Frid.	Satur.
Jan.	1	2	3	4	5	6	7
	8	9	10	11	12	13	14
	15	16	17	18	19	20	21
	22	23	24	25	26	27	28
	29	30	31				
Feb.				1	2	3	4
	5	6	7	8	9	10	11
	12	13	14	15	16	17	18
	19	20	21	22	23	24	25
	26	27	28				
Mar.				1	2	3	4
	5	6	7	8	9	10	11
	12	13	14	15	16	17	18
	19	20	21	22	23	24	25
	26	27	28	29	30	31	
April							1
	2	3	4	5	6	7	8
	9	10	11	12	13	14	15
	16	17	18	19	20	21	22
	23	24	25	26	27	28	29
	30						
May		1	2	3	4	5	6
	7	8	9	10	11	12	13
	14	15	16	17	18	19	20
	21	22	23	24	25	26	27
	28	29	30	31			
June					1	2	3
	4	5	6	7	8	9	10
	11	12	13	14	15	16	17
	18	19	20	21	22	23	24
	25	26	27	28	29	30	

1882	Sund.	Mond.	Tuesd.	Wedn.	Thurs.	Frid.	Satur.
July							1
	2	3	4	5	6	7	8
	9	10	11	12	13	14	15
	16	17	18	19	20	21	22
	23	24	25	26	27	28	29
	30	31					
Aug.			1	2	3	4	5
	6	7	8	9	10	11	12
	13	14	15	16	17	18	19
	20	21	22	23	24	25	26
	27	28	29	30	31		
Sept.						1	2
	3	4	5	6	7	8	9
	10	11	12	13	14	15	16
	17	18	19	20	21	22	23
	24	25	26	27	28	29	30
Oct.	1	2	3	4	5	6	7
	8	9	10	11	12	13	14
	15	16	17	18	19	20	21
	22	23	24	25	26	27	28
	29	30	31				
Nov.				1	2	3	4
	5	6	7	8	9	10	11
	12	13	14	15	16	17	18
	19	20	21	22	23	24	25
	26	27	28	29	30		
Dec.						1	2
	3	4	5	6	7	8	9
	10	11	12	13	14	15	16
	17	18	19	20	21	22	23
	24	25	26	27	28	29	30
	31						

C. G. MEANS.

C. H. MEANS.

C. G. MEANS & SON,

LIVE STOCK

Commission Merchants,

Room 30 Exchange Building,

Kansas City Stock Yards.

www.ingramcontent.com/pod-product-compliance
Lightning Source LLC
Chambersburg PA
CBHW022154020726
47496CB00008B/2702